www.mascotbooks.com

When I Was a Child

For more information, please contact:
Mascot Books
560 Herndon Parkway #120
Herndon, VA 20170
info@mascotbooks.com

CPSIA Code: PRT1116A
Library of Congress Control Number: 2016913877
ISBN-13: 978-1-63177-949-7

Printed in the United States

For my children, Michael, Madison, and Steven.

May you always conquer the fears you encounter.

And a special thanks to my dad, an Italian-American
immigrant, for teaching me that nothing
in life is to be feared;
it is only to be understood.

When I was a child, I was always afraid

Of attics and basements and noises they made.

Each night in my room, when I'd lay down my head,

I thought I heard noises from under my bed.

Outside of my window, the big old oak tree

Would reach out its branches and try to grab me.

The wind became louder when I closed my eyes,

I thought I heard shadows making loud sighs.

When it would rain, there was nothing as frightening

As the sounds and lights of thunder and lightning.

Then one day my dad took me by the hand,

He said he'd explain, so I'd understand.

We went up the rickety, old attic stairs,

And to my surprise, there was nothing there.

The basement, I found, was also not scary.

I didn't see ghosts or monsters so hairy.

Under my bed, where each night I'd hear noise,

To my great surprise, I found some lost toys.

Outside in the daylight, I looked at the tree,
Its branches seemed kind, they were waving at me!

The same creepy wind I heard in the night,
Whistled a tune to the birds in their flight.

Dad said, "When it rains,
think of angels and stars,

Playing together in
lit bumper cars."

I've never forgotten the words that he said,
I've kept them forever, stored safe in my head.

The lesson I learned from my dad on that day
Was that facing your fears, makes them all go away.

About the Author

Michael Cascio is a first generation Italian-American and a graduate of Baruch College. Michael developed a love of poetry at an early age and often writes as a hobby. This book was inspired by the lessons he learned from his dad and those he has passed on to his children. Michael currently lives in New Hyde Park, NY with his wife and children and is a partner in a CPA and Financial Planning firm.